Eva,

I hope you enjoy this
book, and that you know
deep in your heart that
it really is true — I Promise!

Love,
Heather Hodges

— Can you find me on every page?

For Gable, Haven, Emery, and Matalee.
We delight in each one of you.
- K.H. and H.H.

For Caleb and Elijah.
It really is true, I promise.
- H.L.H.

ISBN: 069225191X
ISBN-13: 978-0692251911

I Promise It's True

Written by
Houston and Karen Heflin

Illustrated by
Heather L. Hodges

I went outside to climb a tree
But tore my jeans and scraped my knee.
Do you still love me?

I love you when you laugh,
I love you when you cry,
I love you when you fail,
I love you when you try.

In a race against some friends
I tripped and finished at the end.
Do you still love me?

I love you when you fall,
I love you when you run,
I love you when you've lost,
I love you when you've won.

Today we had a spelling bee.
I couldn't spell "anemone."
Do you still love me?

I love you when you're wrong,
I love you when you're right,
I love you every morning,
I love you every night.

Playing soccer against the wall
I broke a window with the ball.
Do you still love me?

I love you when you're good,
I love you when you're bad,
I love you when you're happy,
I love you when you're sad.

My throat is sore, I can barely speak;
My second school day missed this week.
Do you still love me?

I love you when you're sick,
I love you when you're well,
I love you when you whisper,
I love you when you yell.

I tried to lift it by myself
But the jug of milk slipped off the shelf.
Do you still love me?

I love you when you clean,
I love you when you spill,
I love you when you wiggle,
I love you when you're still.

I wanted to stand in a different place
So the picture shows my grumpy face.
Do you still love me?

I love you when you smile,
I love you when you frown,
I love you when you're up,
I love you when you're down.

I promise it's true.
There's nothing you could do
To make me stop
Loving you.

The End

30196873R00022

Made in the USA
Columbia, SC
31 October 2018